STEPHANIE TRUE PETERS *Illustrated by* ROBERT PAPP

Rumble Tum

DUTTON CHILDREN'S BOOKS

DUTTON CHILDREN'S BOOKS
A division of Penguin Young Readers Group
Published by the Penguin Group
Penguin Group (USA) Inc., 375 Hudson Street, New York, New York 10014, U.S.A.
Penguin Group (Canada), 90 Eglinton Avenue East, Suite 700, Toronto, Ontario M4P 2Y3, Canada
(a division of Pearson Penguin Canada Inc.)
Penguin Books Ltd, 80 Strand, London WC2R 0RL, England
Penguin Ireland, 25 St Stephen's Green, Dublin 2, Ireland (a division of Penguin Books Ltd)
Penguin Group (Australia), 250 Camberwell Road, Camberwell, Victoria 3124, Australia
(a division of Pearson Australia Group Pty Ltd)
Penguin Books India Pvt Ltd, 11 Community Centre, Panchsheel Park, New Delhi - 110 017, India
Penguin Group (NZ), 67 Apollo Drive, Rosedale, North Shore 0632, New Zealand
(a division of Pearson New Zealand Ltd)
Penguin Books (South Africa) (Pty) Ltd, 24 Sturdee Avenue, Rosebank, Johannesburg 2196, South Africa
Penguin Books Ltd, Registered Offices: 80 Strand, London WC2R 0RL, England

Text copyright © 2009 by Stephanie True Peters
Illustrations copyright © 2009 by Robert Papp

Published in the United States by Dutton Children's Books,
a division of Penguin Young Readers Group
345 Hudson Street, New York, New York 10014
www.penguin.com/youngreaders

Designed by Irene Vandervoort

Manufactured in China   First Edition

ISBN 978-0-525-42156-6

1 3 5 7 9 10 8 6 4 2

For Dan,
a dog person who loves our two cats anyway
—S.T.P.

For all the furry four-legged ones
who rumble and tumble and stumble into our lives
—R. P.

When Beth first held her kitten, all she could say was, "Oh, I love, *love*, LOVE you!"

The kitten purred in Beth's arms.

"I've got a great name for her," Beth said. "Rumble Tum!"

"I like it," said Jackson.

"See you soon, Rumble Tum!" Dr. Hale said.

Back home in the playroom, Beth poured kitten food into a bowl. "I bet you're hungry!"

Jackson ran to get water.

"I have some toys for you. And I put your litter box in the closet, for privacy," Beth said. "Come see."

"Look, she wants to play!"
Mom rolled a pom-pom ball.
Rumble Tum pounced.

Beth dangled a string. Rumble Tum
leaped.

Jackson scratched a paper bag.
Rumble Tum dove inside—

and the game started again.

Watching her play, all Beth could think was, *Oh, I love,*
love, LOVE you!

After dinner, Dad read them a story. Rumble Tum read along and looked at the pictures.

Before long, it was time to go to sleep. But Rumble Tum had other ideas.

After lights-out, Rumble Tum set out to find the kitchen.

In the morning, Beth searched all over for the kitten.
She finally found her, safe and sound, snug and asleep.
She found the broom and the dustpan, too.

For the rest of the day, Rumble Tum
was busy. She discovered playthings...

and cozy spots.

She learned how to say
she was hungry...

and to use her sharp claws.

Mom learned to clip those claws to keep them a little less sharp.

Afterward, all Beth could whisper was, "Oh, I love, *love*, LOVE you!"

That week, Beth and Jackson took turns
bringing friends by to meet Rumble Tum. One
afternoon, their next-door neighbor brought
a surprise—at least, Rumble Tum seemed
surprised!

"Mind your manners!" Beth scolded.

Rumble Tum did, and by the day's end, she
had her own friend.

As the days passed, Rumble Tum grew longer and stronger.

She could jump higher and run faster.

And she definitely took up more space.

"It's time for Rumble Tum to visit Dr. Hale," Mom said one morning.

Rumble Tum didn't mind the exam ... but she didn't like the car rides at all.

As they drove home, all Beth could murmur was, "Oh, I love, *love*, LOVE you!"

Two days later, Beth and Rumble Tum played one of their favorite games.

Mom said, "I have an idea. Why don't you play outside?"

Beth opened the front door and saw dark clouds up in the sky. "It's going to rain!" she said.

Suddenly, something small and furry brushed past her feet and out the door. "Rumble Tum! Come back!"

Beth ran after her kitten. Rumble Tum ran faster. She darted under the bushes and then to the tree and then past the fence and then—then there was a flash of lightning!

Beth squeezed her eyes shut. Just for a second. But when she opened them, Rumble Tum was gone.

"Mom, come quick! Rumble Tum is missing!"

Mom came quick. So did Dad and Jackson. They searched
until the rain drove them back into the house.

Inside, all Beth could do was cry.

Finally, the rain stopped.

"Where did you last see her?" Mom asked.

"Over there!"

Beth rushed to the fence. She spotted an open door.

She ran to it and pushed it wide open.

And then she saw her kitten.
Safe and sound, snug and asleep.

Beth scooped Rumble Tum up in her arms.

As her kitten purred, Beth couldn't say a word.

But her heart sang out loud and clear.

"Oh, I love, *love*, LOVE you!"